Simona's Search

by Martín Zimmerman

No one shall make any changes in this title(s) for the purpose of production. No part of this book may be reproduced, stored in a retrieval system, scanned, uploaded, or transmitted in any form, by any means, now known or yet to be invented, including mechanical, electronic, digital, photocopying, recording, videotaping, or otherwise, without the prior written permission of the publisher. No one shall share this title(s), or any part of this title(s), through any social media or file hosting websites.

For all inquiries regarding motion picture, television, online/digital and other media rights, please contact Concord Theatricals Corp.

MUSIC AND THIRD-PARTY MATERIALS USE NOTE

Licensees are solely responsible for obtaining formal written permission from copyright owners to use copyrighted music and/or other copyrighted third-party materials (e.g. artworks, logos) in the performance of this play and are strongly cautioned to do so. If no such permission is obtained by the licensee, then the licensee must use only original music and materials that the licensee owns and controls. Licensees are solely responsible and liable for clearances of all third-party copyrighted materials, including without limitation music, and shall indemnify the copyright owners of the play(s) and their licensing agent, Concord Theatricals Corp., against any costs, expenses, losses and liabilities arising from the use of such copyrighted third-party materials by licensees. For music, please contact the appropriate music licensing authority in your territory for the rights to any incidental music.

IMPORTANT BILLING AND CREDIT REQUIREMENTS

If you have obtained performance rights to this title, please refer to your licensing agreement for important billing and credit requirements.

SIMONA'S SEARCH was originally commissioned by La Jolla Playhouse, (Artistic Director, Christopher Ashley; Managing Director, Michael S. Rosenberg) in La Jolla, California. *SIMONA'S SEARCH* premiered on January 18, 2024 at Connecticut's Hartford Stage. The production was directed by Melia Bensussen, with choreography by Shura Baryshnikov, casting direction by Alaine Alldaffer, scenic design by Yu Shibagaki, costume design by Olivera Gajic, lighting design by Aja M. Jackson, sound design by Aubrey Dube, co-sound design and original music by Lucas Clopton, and projection design by Yana Biryukova. The production stage manager was Nicole Wiegert, and the assistant stage manager was Julius Cruz. The cast was as follows:

SIMONA . . . . .Alejandra Escalante
PAPI . . . . .Al Rodrigo
JAKE . . . . .Christopher Bannow

CHARACTERS

SIMONA – early to mid-30s, Latina.
PAPI / ADVISER – Simona's father, mid-50s to early 60s, Latino.
JAKE / DOCTOR – early 30s.

SETTING

Simona's childhood home, a hospital, and other locations.

TIME

The present.

AUTHOR'S NOTES

Notes on Production

1) Scene numbers are only for the purpose of dividing the play for rehearsal. In production, the scenes should flow seamlessly into one another.
2) It's OK for there to be whimsy despite the play's heavy subject matter. In fact, the subject matter probably makes some whimsy all the more essential.
3) The best version of Simona's narration isn't one which is presentational, one in which she seems to already have the answers and the story figured out. The best version is the one in which she's putting the pieces together and figuring things out in front of us.

One

(**SIMONA** *alone in the space.*)

(*She holds a composition-style notebook in her hands. She opens it, starts writing in it. As she does, her writing appears projected on the scrim...*)

It starts – as it always does – with a story...

SIMONA. A little girl wants nothing more than to host her first sleepover.

(**PAPI** *appears. And immediately has questions.*)

PAPI. Where will everyone sleep?

SIMONA. Her gruff-but-affectionate father isn't opposed to sleepovers in all forms...

PAPI. Our apartment's half the size of your friends' houses.

SIMONA. He's more than happy to let his daughter sleep over at all of her friends' houses...

PAPI. You want everyone squished together like balls in the funhouse?

SIMONA. But the thought of hosting one himself seems... overwhelming.

PAPI. And we only have the one bathroom. You know how girls can be about the bathroom.

Are *you* going to be the one to tell Susie she needs to get out of there already? Because it's not going to be me.

SIMONA.   Unfortunately for him...hosting is precisely what his daughter wants most.

PAPI.   Besides, it's just the two of us, *mi vida*. Your friends have two parents, one to help with the hosting while the other one cooks.

SIMONA.   For as long as this little girl can remember, she has had an uncanny ability to sense the unstated needs of everyone around her.

> (Then **PAPI** *starts searching furiously for something he's misplaced.*)

PAPI.   Simona, have you seen my...my...

SIMONA.   To anticipate what everyone wants before they're even sure they want it.

> (*And suddenly he can't remember what it is he's looking for.*)

PAPI.   Now what was it I was...?

You see what all this sleepover talk is doing to me, Simona?

SIMONA.   You're already wearing your apron, Papi.

> (**PAPI** *looks down, sees* **SIMONA** *is right.*)

PAPI.   Huh. So I am.

SIMONA.   The girl has never stopped to think where her gift came from. She's just always had it. And what good is a gift if it's not put to use?

So she draws up charts of possible sleeping arrangements.

> (**SIMONA** *hands* **PAPI** *a chart. He furrows his brow at it.*)

PAPI.   What am I looking at here?

SIMONA. She drafts menus with plans for how she can help prepare them.

> (**PAPI** *keeps spinning the chart around, trying to make sense of it.* **SIMONA** *keeps handing him more papers.*)

She buries her father with so many answers to each of his objections that he finally has no choice but to say:

PAPI. Alright. We can do it.

But everyone goes to sleep the second I say so.

SIMONA. The second condition is one she's heard her whole life…

PAPI. And absolutely no one in my bedroom after I've gone to sleep. Only knock if it's an emergency, OK?

SIMONA. The girl squeals with delight, and immediately starts dreaming up the various games the partygoers could play.

Phone calls are made, invitations sent, the girl can hardly sleep in the weeks leading up to the night.

Her father, for his part, does his very best to help.

Even though the girl finds some of how he does quietly embarrassing.

Like how he insists on cooking instead of ordering pizza.

And those little pastries he serves instead of ice cream?

You know. The strangely-spiced ones from his homeland?

> (**PAPI** *presents a platter to the audience.*)

PAPI. Try it first before you say you don't like it…

SIMONA. The girl works hard to stifle her embarrassment at her friends' suspicious faces when they sink their teeth into them.

But she stifles it for her father, because she's a good daughter. And because she sees how taxing it was for him to make her special night happen.

Then, at the agreed-upon hour, her father heads off to bed.

Only the girls are too giddy to even think about sleeping. And soon the most headstrong guest decides that every closed door in the apartment is an insult. A *challenge.*

And even though the host's father was very clear about his rules, it goes against every fiber of her being to say no to her guests.

So she indulges the partygoers as they tip-toe about the entire apartment like inmates about to stage a prison break. Into the bathroom, the closets, the kitchen, and finally...

The bedroom with the slumbering man inside it.

> (**PAPI** *appears in silhouette, snoring, mouth agape, large aquiline nose piercing the air.*)

As the entire group stands there, staring at the snoring man – his oversized nose and open mouth – everyone seems disappointed that something more exciting wasn't waiting for them on the other side of the door. The ringleader comments on how much he looks like her grandpa. She wonders aloud why he looks so old, and the host doesn't have an answer because to her he doesn't look old at all.

To her, he just looks like Papi.

To keep the disappointed crowd from turning on her, the little instigator ups the ante. She climbs on the bed, and cups one hand over the man's open mouth while pinching his nose with the other.

> *(We see the silhouette of a girl do as she describes to* **PAPI**'s *own silhouette.)*

> *(***PAPI*** *violently jerks awake.)*

> *(And sends the little girl's silhouette floating through the air...)*

No one will soon forget the thwack of her little body against the opposite wall.

A thwack that immediately awakens the man so he can see what he's done.

From there, things unravel fast.

The room is vacated, the door slammed, a flurry of phone calls made, and next thing anyone knows, parents have arrived to question the father.

And the little host?

She sits silently at the door to her father's room

hand pressed to the wood

hoping for some explanation

some ammunition against the mounting accusations.

Until the police arrive and ask her to step back so they can pry the door open...

That's when she sees the sight that probably saves her father from jail time or a long string of lawsuits.

The girl's father is crouched, shivering

clutching himself in the middle of the floor.

> *(We see* **PAPI** *in silhouette, as described.)*

He's ringed by a shallow pool of his own urine.

The police shut the door an instant later

shut the door for years on any insight the girl might have into her father's breakdown

but the sight of her father huddled on the floor sears itself into her memory.

    (**PAPI**'s *silhouette quickly fades from view.*)

And all the more because of how her father handles it

– or doesn't handle it –

when the girl wakes up the next day.

Two

> (**PAPI** *appears – in person – armed with brochures. Kind of like the man who opens up his trench coat to reveal hundreds of watches? Yeah. Exactly like that. Except it's brochures.*)

PAPI. I'm thinking we can start at the Natural History Museum!

> (*She keeps writing in the notebook. Again her writing appears in projection…*)

A confounding – and illuminating – reaction

And then work our way toward aerospace and then maybe the planetarium!

SIMONA. What follows is a whirlwind of a day.

PAPI. Unless you'd like to do it the other way! Then cap off at the science center!

SIMONA. A day that would be any inquisitive child's fantasy.

PAPI. If a woolly mammoth and elephant met do you think they'd recognize each other? Call each other cousins?

SIMONA. A day the little girl has lived a hundred times.

PAPI. To think that the strongest species on earth is a tiny little microscopic guy that's survived millions of years! And could even survive in outer space!

SIMONA. Because as long as she could remember

her father was always shuttling her to one museum or another

pilfering magazines from the city college science departments inundating her with information about the great mysteries of the universe.

> (**PAPI** *quickly shuts his coat and opens it again. As if by magic, all the brochures have been replaced by science magazines and meticulously clipped and highlighted articles.*)

That her father does the same on this day

keeps his gaze fixed firmly on the stars

on "the big questions"

instead of on himself...

> (*He begins plucking the articles from his coat one by one...*)

...makes the little girl question so many things she'd just accepted about her father...

> (*...And efficiently and expertly tapes them together into a little booklet which he unfurls before her like an accordion.*)

Like how he insists they walk everywhere but never take the same route twice.

> (*And suddenly he takes off walking!*)

PAPI. God I love grids!

> (*And turning unexpectedly at sharp right angles.*)

SIMONA. A habit which has led the little girl to instinctively watch the direction of her father's feet. So she doesn't find her shoulder suddenly yanked out of socket.

PAPI. You know what's the best thing about a grid? There are infinite ways to get from one place to the next!

SIMONA. Or her father's menagerie of friends…

PAPI. Frank!

José my man! How is the life treating you!

SIMONA. Friends he drops in on by surprise while walking between the many laundromats he manages for a living.

PAPI. Victor, you should've seen this documentary they had about Hubble telescope on the TV last night. To think all it's seen. Unfathomable. You can try all you like, but you just cannot fathom it, my friend.

SIMONA. Friends he knows everything about…

PAPI. You still getting your son that skateboard for his birthday? Or did your wife talk you out of it?

SIMONA. …but who know nothing about her father. Who have never even set foot inside his home.

And most devastating of all

is the realization that she knows even less about her father than his friends do.

Like…why he came to this country

or why he never bothered teaching her his native language of Spanish

and instead insisted on her taking French.

Her father's been too busy inundating her with questions of his own.

PAPI. So. What was your favorite part of the museum? The asteroids? Or the telescope?

SIMONA. And the fact that she's allowed him to distract her like this floods the little girl with guilt.

PAPI. You going to tell me all about your presentation in math today?

SIMONA. A guilt that keeps her from caring that all her friends stop inviting her to *their* sleepovers...

PAPI. And what about science? When do you start the chemistry unit?

SIMONA. *(To* **PAPI.***)* Papi?

PAPI. Yes, *mi vida*?

> *(The slightest hesitation.)*

SIMONA. I was just wondering...if maybe we could go to the library on Saturday?

> *(He beams at this suggestion.)*

PAPI. Of course, *mi vida*...why would you even have to ask?

SIMONA. Her search for answers begins with the history of his homeland.

And after some simple arithmetic

she realizes what probably caused her father's flight

that it probably caused so much more

so she absorbs everything she can about his country

every book

or cassette she can get her hands on

devours them wholesale...

> *(She throws on headphones, starts singing to herself in Spanish...what she lacks in skill she makes up for in enthusiasm...*)*

PAPI. *(Offstage.)* Simona...?

(**SIMONA** *keeps singing, oblivious.*)

(Entering.) Simona, I said dinner's ready –

(He stops in his tracks when he sees his embarrassed daughter holding a Walkman.)

(Caught in the act, she immediately presses stop, pulls off the headphones.)

I thought we agreed. No music until homework's finished –

SIMONA. It helps me concentrate.

PAPI. Didn't look like it.

(No answer.)

Maybe I should listen? See if I agree?

(She tentatively hands over the Walkman.)

(As he slips on the headphones, presses play...)

(We hear the song she was singing. A folk song. A protest song from another era. The audio is crackly. The melody, haunting. The rhythm, dogged, determined.)*

(**PAPI** *sits there, stunned...until he violently rips off the headphones. Tries to catch his breath...then covers quickly.*)

Where'd you get it?

SIMONA. The library.

---

* A license to produce *Simona's Search* does not include a performance license for any third-party or copyrighted recordings. Licensees should create their own.

PAPI. I should write them a letter. About wasting funds on...frivolity.

(She nods, chastened.)

You're better off listening to Bach. Math in musical form.

SIMONA. From that moment forward she takes an even more furtive approach to her investigation:

Three

A Field Study of the Possible Symptoms of Trauma...

(**SIMONA** *sits opposite* **PAPI** *at the table while he reads science articles.*)

(*She writes furtively in her notebook.*)

1) Alexithymia = Inability to describe feelings

SIMONA. Why don't we play a game?

PAPI. *(Intrigued.)* What sort of game?

SIMONA. Why don't we call it... "What if?"

PAPI. You mean like what if the universe were collapsing instead of expanding? Or what if we lived in the time when the sun was about to blow into a supernova and had to escape the solar system in order to survive?

SIMONA. Not...exactly. A little more realistic what if.

PAPI. So like what if we developed gills and could live underwater.

SIMONA. More like we take turns describing a bunch of real world scenarios...

PAPI. *(Hiding his disappointment.)* Oh.

SIMONA. ...and the other one describes how they think that scenario would make them feel.

PAPI. What do you mean "make them feel?"

SIMONA. Like...what feelings they would have? –

PAPI. I understand the words you're saying, *mi vida*, I speak *English*... I just don't understand the point.

SIMONA. The point is that it's a game. That it's fun.

PAPI. Doesn't sound fun to me.

SIMONA. Well you can't know until you've tried it.

(He says nothing.)

OK, I'll go first. Imagine…you're standing on the street where you grew up…and you're watching a bulldozer demolish your childhood home.

PAPI. But I wouldn't be standing there.

SIMONA. Say you were.

PAPI. But I wouldn't. Why would I just be standing there in front of a building when a wrecking ball's about to go into it? I could get hit by debris.

SIMONA. Say you were standing at a safe distance…

PAPI. Well I wouldn't be.

SIMONA. Papi –

PAPI. You're the one who wanted to play what if. So I'm telling you. The what if is I wouldn't be standing there. The what if is I would run.

SIMONA. Well say you couldn't. Or you were in a magical glass ball in the sky where you knew you wouldn't get hurt. And you were watching your childhood home be bulldozed.

How would watching that make you feel?

(Brief pause.)

PAPI. I don't know how I would feel. So I guess that's my answer: I don't know.

SIMONA. That's not an answer.

PAPI. It is for me.

SIMONA. Can you at least try?

PAPI. Why?

SIMONA. Because we're playing a game, Papi.

PAPI. Well it's a stupid game. And I don't like it.

(He goes back to reading his article.)

(And she quietly writes something in her notebook.)

1A) Other signs of Alexithymia; Patient is unaware of illness, and struggles to describe physical symptoms

*(**PAPI** shuffles about the apartment in his slippers, performing some quotidian task. Chopping vegetables, washing dishes, or the like.)*

(He is visibly sluggish, unwell...)

*(When **SIMONA** enters.)*

SIMONA. Are you feeling alright?

PAPI. I'm fine. Why wouldn't I be?

SIMONA. You're sweating bullets.

PAPI. Am I?

(He wipes his forehead.)

Someone must've turned up the heat.

SIMONA. I just turned it down.

(She approaches him...)

PAPI. What are you –?

(...And puts a hand on his forehead.)

SIMONA. You're burning up. Does anything else hurt?

PAPI. Why would anything hurt if I'm telling you I feel fine?

SIMONA. Well, you're clearly not fine, Mr. Grumpy Pants –

PAPI. I am *not* grumpy –

SIMONA. – so you might as well try and tell me what hurts.

PAPI. I just told you nothing...

(He's a little light-headed.)

...nothing...

(Suddenly he's overcome with a coughing fit.)

2) An aversion to close physical contact

SIMONA. Papi!

*(She runs up to greet **PAPI** with a big bear hug...)*

(When he stops her short, with an extended hand, as if for a handshake.)

(Ding.)

Or unexpected touch

(He's washing the dishes when she approaches from behind...)

(But he startles well before she can even come close to reaching him.)

(Ding.)

3) Irregular or Asymmetrical Gait (For victims of repeated physical trauma)

(**SIMONA** *and* **PAPI** *walk en route to some destination.*)

(*A museum, probably. Isn't it always a museum?*)

(*She suddenly stops...*)

(*And he – with his hyperactive startle reflex – immediately wheels around to see why.*)

SIMONA. I just need to tie my shoe real quick.

Why don't you go grab us a spot in line. I'll be right behind you.

(*As he continues ahead, she kneels down as if to tie her shoe...*)

(*And surreptitiously pulls out a notebook...*)

(*Which she uses to write down observations while she studies his gait from afar...*)

(*As she writes, her scribbled notes appear in projection...*)

Lists to the right while he walks...

Left foot comes off the ground a great deal more than his right...

Arms hang limp, motionless, as if they're pinned to his sides...

(*Then, suddenly he freezes. And she looks at him, stuck in that most peculiar of positions.*)

Four

SIMONA. This is how the not-so-little girl comes to realize her father was almost certainly tortured and starts linking each peculiarity of her father's gait

with the precise methods of torture his government used.

To try and unlock the details of his past.

But all this does is bring her to the intersection of infinite possibility

and searing specificity

filling her head with countless hypotheticals

any of which could be true

so in her head all of them are true.

> *(A Dark Figure steps into the space. The edges of his silhouetted form are almost on fire.)*

This is when the nightmares begin.

She sees a man in silhouette, a Dark Figure, hovering over her.

She knows this Dark Figure to be her father's torturer.

The man visits her night after night and enacts a bloody ritual on her body.

> *(The Dark Figure moves toward her slowly, deliberately.)*

> *(As he does, he slowly raises an instrument of torture.)*

> *(What it is we can't tell. But its jagged silhouette is awe-inspiring, terrifying.)*

And yet for all the terror this man brings into her life

she has this sense that if she could just see him clearly

if she could just fill in the contours of that silhouette…

> *(She slips on her headphones, plays the folk
> song while she stares at the Dark Figure to see
> if that helps…*)*

(Staring at the Dark Figure.) So she delves deeper into
her investigations

while continuing to excel in math and science

and make her papi proud amidst his unrelenting
attention…

All of which leaves little time for anything like fun

or friends

there will always be time for that later, she keeps telling
herself…

And she vows to delve even deeper into her
investigations when she gets to college…

> *(Just as the Dark Figure is about to reach
> her…)*

> *(And bring his instrument of torture down
> onto her…)*

> *(The lights flash.)*

---

* A license to produce *Simona's Search* does not include a performance
license for any third-party or copyrighted recordings. Licensees should
create their own.

Five

(Papers. Endless piles of papers. Enough to bury a man alive. But despite the overwhelming chaos there does appear to be some system – some logic to how they're sorted. Though what that logic is we can't possibly glean.)

(Into this madness steps **SIMONA**, *suitcase in tow.)*

SIMONA. Papi?

(No answer.)

Papi, are you in here –?

*(**PAPI** pokes his head out from behind the piles of papers.)*

PAPI. What are you doing here?

SIMONA. You didn't get my message? Left it last week? Said I'd be home today?

PAPI. Wait, why – Is something the matter?

SIMONA. Fall break?

PAPI. So soon?

SIMONA. Someone must've missed me.

PAPI. Of course I missed you – all I did was miss you...

(Gesturing to the articles.)

...can't you tell?

(She does her best to feign a smile as he clutches her shoulders, sizes her up.)

Let's have a look, let's have a look...

(Giving her a long, hard stare.)

You certainly look smarter.

SIMONA. I'm not sure I feel smarter...

PAPI. Humility is the first sign of intelligence.

SIMONA. Says who?

PAPI. One of these articles here somewhere...

(He searches in vain for a moment...)

But just because you're learning all these new things doesn't mean your old man's too slow to keep up. And it doesn't mean I'm going to let you squirm out of discussing them with me. Chaos theory and quantum mechanics and oh there was this fascinating one on string theory –

SIMONA. If those are the same ones you've been mailing me –

PAPI. Of course I know you haven't had time. This is why I made copies. For when you're on break. So you can talk about an article or two while you're home. Give your old man the benefit of your newly-acquired knowledge.

SIMONA. I'm not sure how much knowledge I could've acquired...

PAPI. Seven weeks of university is seven weeks more than I ever had. And more than enough time for your mind to bloom!

SIMONA. But it's not like I was... I mean, I didn't take any actual classes in...

PAPI. You didn't?

(She says nothing.)

Of course you didn't. They make you take all the stupid perquisites.

SIMONA. Prerequisites.

PAPI. That's not what I said?

SIMONA. Perquisites are good stuff you get without having to do anything else. Prerequisites are the bad stuff you have to do before you get any good stuff.

PAPI. So they're pretty much the same word except they mean the exact opposite?

SIMONA. *(She can't help but smile.)* Pretty much.

PAPI. Well, you're smart to get them out of the way now – the perquisites – so that way when it comes time to take the classes that really matter you can give your whole mind over to them.

SIMONA. You really didn't get my message?

(She gets up to check the message machine.)

PAPI. What does it matter if all you said was that you're going to be home?

(Beat.)

SIMONA. I might have also said something about not taking physics.

PAPI. Because of the perquisites.

SIMONA. Because... I might not want to study physics.

(Long pause.)

PAPI. What would you study instead?

(Brief pause.)

SIMONA. Neuroscience...and Spanish.

(Beat.)

PAPI. Well…they say it's good for you to explore, no? Stretch your mind? Isn't that what they say the university is for?

>   (*He smiles. A feigned smile. Then starts to gather up the articles.*)

SIMONA. It doesn't mean you have to go throw all the articles away, Papi.

PAPI. I'm just setting them aside until I can create some sort of system to file them for safe keeping. What's important is we have them waiting. In case you change your mind. What's the statistic? Four times the average college student changes their mind about what to study?

SIMONA. And if I'm not average?

PAPI. Of course you're not, *mi vida.* There's no way you ever could be. I'm just saying, what could it hurt to keep the articles around when you only decided last week to –

SIMONA. How do you know when I decided?

PAPI. Huh?

SIMONA. How do you know I didn't decide today?

PAPI. Because you said so.

SIMONA. I never said when I decided.

PAPI. Yes you did. You *just* said –

SIMONA. Unless you did get my message.

>   (*Beat.*)

PAPI. *Ohhhh…*you mean *that* message. Why didn't you say *that* message?

SIMONA. The only message I left.

PAPI. I forgot all about that one. Erased it right away because I thought you were joking with me. "Kidding" like you like to say.

SIMONA. Why would I kid about something like that?

PAPI. Why would you not want to study physics?

> *(Beat.)*

SIMONA. I guess I'm interested in something that feels a little more...relevant?

PAPI. Relevant?

SIMONA. To my life.

PAPI. Who do you know who speaks Spanish?

SIMONA. Besides you?

PAPI. I speak English. You don't need to speak Spanish to speak to me. It's inefficient. And I've already told you I don't have any family left –

SIMONA. I literally know no human beings who speak French.

PAPI. And what about this neuroscience? What about it could be so urgent that you would just give up on answering the big questions?

SIMONA. Answering big questions is exactly what I'm trying to do.

PAPI. Bigger questions than why everything exists, what everything's made of?

SIMONA. How our environment shapes our perception. How our childhood shapes our personality. Or what's going on in our brains when we make a decision or listen to music or remember the past –

PAPI. Since when did *we* become so self-centered? Is that what university does to you?

SIMONA. Or the impact of trauma on the brain. And what can be done to reverse that impact. To help people heal.

(*Pause. With that lingering in the air, they both wonder whether they should touch it.*)

PAPI. And what is it that got you interested in that last question?

Because, you know, normally there is some reason – something that happens in a person's life – that makes them have to ask something so...peculiar. But as far as I can tell you have had a perfectly normal, perfectly happy life.

(*No answer.*)

Unless there's something you're not telling me. Unless you've been secretly miserable all these years –

SIMONA. Of course not.

PAPI. Then what could have happened to you to make you want to ask something so –

SIMONA. Do you really need to ask?

(*Long pause. Something shifts in him.*)

PAPI. I won't let you provoke me.

(*She turns to us.*)

SIMONA. After that briefest peek behind the curtain, her father immediately builds a wall of such hollow enthusiasm for what she's studying...

PAPI. (*Flashing a clenched smile.*) That's so wonderful, *mi vida*!

SIMONA. ...he makes his daughter feel like a bully for even considering confronting him about it...

PAPI. What do you mean I never ask any questions about what you're studying? Aren't I always saying how proud I am of you? And maybe if I don't ask enough questions it's because I'm just not sure what to ask.

SIMONA. All while science articles keep accumulating and accumulating in her room...

> *(The ever-increasing pile of science articles materializes around her.)*

PAPI. Or maybe I'm embarrassed for you to see how stupid I am because I never got to go to university at all, you know, not like you...

SIMONA. Until finding enough space to lie down on her own bed feels about as futile as genuine communication between the two of them...

So her phone calls become rarer and rarer...her visits home almost nonexistent...

Six

SIMONA. And the not-so-little girl tries using college to continue her quest on other fronts.

She tries joining the Latino Student Union

determined to understand that part of herself

but the other students

vault from English to Spanish so effortlessly

acrobatically

it intimidates her.

And when they talk about what it means to be Latino

their stories are always about family

friends

the people they bond with

over music

rituals

food.

But the girl hasn't shared her culture with...anyone

so when they ask her about it

she's not sure what to say.

Suddenly her culture feels like an ill-fitting dress

suddenly she feels ashamed for all those times she went to the library

checked out those cassettes

all the times she's listened to that music thinking it was something she could ever own...

So she stops going to the meetings

stops listening to the music

keeps studying Spanish because it's essential to her search

but other than that?

she narrows her focus

channels all her energy into her studies

and when this just makes her nightmares worse

makes the Dark Figure's contours burn brighter and brighter in her sleep…

…she stops sleeping.

Considers her insomnia a gift.

Uses the extra time to get a job in a lab at school

and win the admiration of all her professors.

She lives for the glow in their eyes each time they say:

PAPI. Excellent work, Simona!

SIMONA. She earns the highest GPA in her major

then a spot in a prestigious grad program

where she nurses her insomnia like it's some secret weapon…

> *(A coffee shop. **SIMONA** sits at a table for two, reads.)*

> *(When another young grad student, **JAKE**, approaches.)*

JAKE. Hey.

> *(She doesn't look up, keeps reading her book. Does she, in her exhaustion, even realize he's there?)*

It's um...pretty late to be reading um...

(He steals a peek at the cover of her book.)

Generational Trauma and its Effects on the Families of Torture Survivors – Whoa. That is some heavy shit.

SIMONA. Huh?

JAKE. Oh. Hi! I was just saying that uh... Once you hit two a.m. it should be like illegal to read something so...

SIMONA. So...?

JAKE. Heavy? Like shouldn't there be a rule that between two a.m. and eight a.m. you can only read like graphic novels or –

SIMONA. Graphic novels?

JAKE. Or...chick-lit?

(She has this look on her face like "what the fuck are you talking about?")

Yeah, I didn't think so.

(She still says nothing.)

I'm Jake. I apologize if I'm interrupting something important, it's just I've seen you here a lot lately and since this happens to be my hang-out as well I thought I'd do the neighborly thing and introduce myself. So... hey.

(A little slow on the uptake with this sort of thing, it suddenly occurs to her what this interaction might be about.)

SIMONA. You have a hard time sleeping too, Jake?

JAKE. Only at night. During the day I can't seem to stop.

SIMONA. So then you're nocturnal?

JAKE. Precisely.

SIMONA. Like a hamster or a house cat?

JAKE. Or a vampire.

Not that I am a vampire. Though of course if I were a vampire would I really be warning you about that ahead of time?

Alas I am a mere mortal. Who's sentenced to wander the underworld with all the other creeps and vagabonds. Until I occasionally bump into someone decent like you.

(On anyone else his shtick might come off as creepy. Or terribly awkward. But he seems to wear it well.)

SIMONA. And what exactly makes you think I'm decent, Jake?

JAKE. Intuition.

SIMONA. Then you should probably get yours checked out 'cause it's in pretty shitty shape.

(She returns to reading her book.)

(He assumes that means the interaction has ended.)

(So he starts off...)

(Until she pushes out the other chair at her table with her leg.)

(The screech of the sliding chair stops him in his tracks.)

(He looks at the chair...at her...)

(She does not look at him.)

(Still, he goes out on a limb, and sits.)

(Which seems to go well for him.)

(Or at least not badly. Since she doesn't shout at him or give him a death-stare or ask him what the fuck he's doing there.)

(She just sits there, reading...)

(Until she looks up from her book to find he's slid her a note...)

Your name?

(Without looking at him, she writes a response, slides it back to him.)

(The instant he opens it...)

(The lights flash.)

(Suddenly he's back at the edge of the space. Bag slung over his shoulder.)

(He scans the room...spots **SIMONA** *seated at the same table. In the other chair this time. Head buried in a book.)*

(He looks at her a long moment. But she does not look up.)

(Not wanting to disturb her, he sets off in search of another seat.)

(But the instant he passes her...she kicks out the other chair for him. Without looking up.)

(As soon as he sits, she slides him an empty notebook. Once again, without looking at him.)

(He looks at it, confused.)

(She takes it back, scribbles...)

Ask me something?

(He reads. Nods. Smiles. Writes.)

(And we see their "conversation" projected behind them...)

SIMONA. They continue like this for weeks

writing intimate details of their lives...

*(**JAKE** speaks aloud as he writes.)*

JAKE. It's only ever been my mom and me. For as long as I can remember. We were always moving around, you know. Like I would never know where we'd be living the next month...

SIMONA. She talks about her American mother, who died in a car accident when she was two...

JAKE. So wherever we were living, I'd retreat to my room – no matter how small it was – I'd just hole myself up in it...and disappear into whatever books I could get my hands on...

SIMONA. But somehow she manages to avoid saying much about her father...

JAKE. But it sounds like you might know a bit about that.

SIMONA. Or rather, writing much about her father...

JAKE. Taking refuge in reading?

SIMONA. Because apart from the subtle glances they take turns stealing at each other across that coffee shop table...their only real communication is what's written in that book...

(Their pattern of behavior repeats, heightens, becomes a subtle choreography of kicked-out chairs...)

(Of notebooks sliding from one hand to another...)

(Of scribbling...)

(Stolen glances...)

(All while the sheer volume of their words starts to overlap on the scrim behind them, filling the scrim with increasing brightness.)

(Until one time when she slides him back the notebook.)

(And as he goes to grab it from her...)

(Their hands touch.)

(Accidentally?)

(She's startled, pulls her hand away...)

(But stops herself. Lets it sit there. Her hand in his.)

(Without making eye contact. Still reading.)

(She smiles a quiet smile. A secret smile.)

(As the scrim behind them – by now almost completely filled with their words – throbs with light.)

(The lights flash.)

(And we find them kissing. Furiously. Passionately.)

(Despite her lack of experience, she's clearly into it. Clearly just as much of an agent in this as he is.)

(But then he backs her up against a wall...)

(And starts kissing down her body.)

(She throws her head back, eyes closed, enjoys this development...)

(But when she opens her eyes, she sees the Dark Figure across the room.)

(She gasps.)

JAKE. Everything alright?

SIMONA. *(Covering.)* Yeah, no, fine, great.

(She quickly shuts her eyes, desperate not to betray her panic, desperate to not let it spoil the moment.)

(But the instant she opens them again, the Dark Figure is there. Brandishing his instrument of torture.)

*(She immediately grabs **JAKE**, pulls him to his feet.)*

JAKE. What's the matter? You don't like –?

SIMONA. No, I do, I do, I just –

(She pushes him against the wall, starts going to work on him as best she can.)

(And the whole encounter turns into this strange, unintentional, dance of control.)

(She tries to take the lead, to be the active one, the one on top, but every time he tries to give her pleasure – and we can tell he genuinely <u>wants</u> to give her pleasure – every time his efforts to do so make her physically prone in any way...)

(The Dark Figure appears.)

*(And **SIMONA** has to shield her mounting panic.)*

(And yet she doesn't want to disappoint him. She clearly really likes him.)

(So eventually she gives in. Lets him take control.)

(And just tries to go deep, bury her fear, until he finishes...)

(And falls asleep on top of her.)

(As she lays beneath him, the Dark Figure hovers over her. And she looks paralyzed with fear.)

(Eventually the best she can do is quietly slip out from under him, and retreat to a corner, where she cries.)

Seven

SIMONA. For the first time since she turned ten and caught that glimpse of her father through his cracked bedroom door

she stops investigating her father's past.

She hides her notes

locks them away

in the hopes that she can banish the Dark Figure for good.

For the first time since she can remember

she spends days without thinking of her father

his past

even once.

Then

and only then

does she try again with Jake.

> (*He appears. More kissing, fondling.*)

> (*Even more giddy excitement this time.*)

> (*But once again, as soon as she's pinned beneath his weight...*)

> (*The Dark Figure appears.*)

> (*She gets up and walks across the room while* **JAKE** *continues thrusting into the empty space where she was.*)

> (*She sits in the corner and knits while he continues.*)

(Not that this banishes the Dark Figure altogether.)

(But it seems to make him smaller.)

(More manageable.)

JAKE. *(To the empty spot where she was.)* Everything OK?

SIMONA. *(Focused on her knitting.)* Yeah, no, it's wonderful. Why wouldn't it be?

> *(He continues thrusting into the empty space while she knits. The clicking of of her knitting needles grows louder – an attempt to drown out the insistent rhythm of his thrusts.)*

> *(Until he stops.)*

JAKE. I know they say you're like...not supposed to ask...

SIMONA. Ask...?

JAKE. How you're doing? Or how you've done? That that's like a cardinal sin of sex or something – asking how you were – so I'm probably like going to be banished to sexual hell for even thinking about bringing it up in the middle of –

SIMONA. You're not.

JAKE. I just want to make sure there's not...something else I can be doing. You know, to...make sure you're having a good time?

SIMONA. I am having a good time. I'm having a great time.

JAKE. I just...feel like maybe we're not really connected right now.

Like you're...somewhere else. Like you've been somewhere else the last several times we've...

SIMONA. But I'm right here.

JAKE. I don't mean physically, I just mean...

(She looks at him, says nothing.)

You know what. Just forget it. Forget I even said anything. It's probably just in my head and...this is why the rule exists probably. Because one person gets paranoid and then they say something that has absolutely zero basis in reality but then saying it aloud makes it real, and no matter how hard each of them tries, neither of them can get it out of their heads –

SIMONA. I appreciate your bringing it up. I do.

JAKE. I just want to make sure I'm doing everything I can, you know? To connect.

(As he says these words, she can't help but stare at the Dark Figure, who still lingers silently in the background.)

Don't you want that, too?

SIMONA. Of course I do.

(The lights flash.)

Eight

(Simona's grad school **ADVISER** *appears where the Dark Figure was.)*

ADVISER. Simona. I'm really glad you asked to meet. I had actually been meaning to have a chat with you.

(With a chuckle.)

No need to look frightened. Just wanted to check in. Make sure the other grad students aren't hazing you too badly.

SIMONA. Not at all, Dr. Gardner.

ADVISER. Please. Mitch.

SIMONA. They've been more than welcoming.

ADVISER. And how about you? You getting enough sleep?

SIMONA. Most important eight hours of the day.

ADVISER. Sleep's usually the first thing a young grad student cuts back on. Which is a sign they're in over their head.

SIMONA. Right.

ADVISER. It's only going to be an uphill climb from here. And if you're already struggling to sleep, well...you might as well get out now. While you're still young enough to go down a different path.

(In certain moments, we think we might actually hear **PAPI***'s accent creeping into the* **ADVISER***'s speech.)*

SIMONA. I'm getting plenty of sleep, Mitch.

ADVISER. I knew you would be. We have high hopes for you, Simona. It's not often we take a risk on someone straight out of undergrad, but I believe you are a special case.

SIMONA. I certainly hope so.

ADVISER. Now what was it you wanted to discuss?

SIMONA. I wanted to run a possible research topic by you. One that I think could be the basis for a larger line of inquiry. Perhaps even a thesis.

ADVISER. How exciting that you're already latching onto a thesis topic!

SIMONA. I guess I'm wondering if you know of anyone who's encountered any evidence of...the children of trauma sufferers also...experiencing some of the same symptoms as their parents. Even though they themselves have never experienced any trauma.

ADVISER. If you're talking about secondary effects, such as a paranoid parent who suffered trauma generating an anxiety disorder in the child –

SIMONA. No, I mean...primary symptoms. Of the initial traumatic event.

ADVISER. *(Puzzled.)* What sort of primary symptoms?

SIMONA. Well...let's say the child seems to have some sort of traumatic memory of events they never lived. Such as a sudden, debilitating fear of being made immobile or an aversion to unexpected physical contact.

ADVISER. I think those are easily explained as secondary effects –

SIMONA. But what if the child is absolutely certain that the symptoms they're experiencing are not in any way rooted in how their parent treated them?

ADVISER. They could be fabricated memories. The parent tells you in detail what's happened –

SIMONA. Except the parent hasn't told.

ADVISER. How can you know?

SIMONA. Let's just assume for a second that I do.

(Beat.)

ADVISER. Then I believe you're describing hallucinations. And if you'd like to explore whether children of trauma sufferers have an elevated risk of hallucinations –

SIMONA. That's not...what I'm talking about.

ADVISER. Then what are you talking about, Simona? And why are you being so stubborn with me about it?

SIMONA. I'm just...trying to make myself understood.

ADVISER. You're sure this doesn't have anything to do with your personal history? I know your interest in trauma is personal. And if some of the things you're describing to me are things you yourself have experienced...

Let's just say I hope you'd have the presence of mind to seek professional help.

(He slides her a card.)

Dr. Emery has decades of experience dealing with this sort of thing. It would be great if the two of you could connect.

(As soon as she takes the card, the lights flash.)

(And suddenly her **ADVISER** *has become a* **PSYCHIATRIST**.*)*

(Perhaps the barest trace of a Viennese accent bleeds in and out of the **PSYCHIATRIST***'s speech. Just enough to make us wonder if it's actually there.)*

PSYCHIATRIST. Tell me more about these hallucinations you've been having.

SIMONA. I...never said anything about –

PSYCHIATRIST. Mitch reached out to me.

SIMONA. He did?

PSYCHIATRIST. Seemed very concerned about your well-being.

> *(Beat.)*

SIMONA. They're not hallucinations, Dr. Emery. They're memories.

PSYCHIATRIST. Visceral, physical memories is how he said you described them.

SIMONA. Yes.

PSYCHIATRIST. Of events you've never experienced.

> *(She says nothing.)*

It's not possible to remember something that hasn't happened to you, Simona.

SIMONA. But I...know what hallucinations are – I mean, I study...and I know these are not –

PSYCHIATRIST. Do you have a family history of schizophrenia?

SIMONA. Um...excuse me?

PSYCHIATRIST. Your family history.

SIMONA. I...don't really know my family history –

PSYCHIATRIST. *(Writing.)* It sounds as if there's at least some mental illness...

SIMONA. Did you just say...schizophrenia?

PSYCHIATRIST. You're squarely within the age range of onset. And the stress of something like...say, the first semester of grad school, is often a trigger. You have no idea how many students your age I see with this.

SIMONA. ...

PSYCHIATRIST. Now have you noticed any patterns as to what precedes the hallucinations?

SIMONA. I just told you they're not –

PSYCHIATRIST. It's nothing to be ashamed of, Simona. I know there's a lot of stigma around the S-word. But you're going to have to let it go. You potentially have a very serious problem, and you're never going to overcome it if you refuse to acknowledge it exists.

>　*(Beat.)*

SIMONA. May I um...use your bathroom?

PSYCHIATRIST. *(Taking notes.)* Down the hall, third door on your right.

>　*(She gets up, clearly shaken...looks over her shoulder...and takes off. Once she's far enough, she tears up the card for the psychiatrist that her adviser handed her...)*

Nine

*(...Then **JAKE** appears across the space as the Dark Figure looms in the background.)*

*(**SIMONA** races to **JAKE**, kisses him deeply, fully. She almost seems tipsy.)*

JAKE. *(Taken aback – but not in a bad way.)* Hey.

SIMONA. That's my apology.

JAKE. For?

SIMONA. Not calling. Not returning your calls.

JAKE. It's totally fine –

SIMONA. I had a bunch of deadlines I got behind on and I just got this insane tunnel vision and I'm so sorry and I promise it won't happen again and I have to be honest that I'm a little new at this whole balancing work and love thing –

JAKE. Love?

(She thinks about that a moment, smiles. They both just let that hang in the air.)

You finished them? The deadlines?

(Her smile increases. She nods.)

(He pulls out a notebook. Their notebook. Full of their shared written history.)

I was...I guess you could say I was missing you – us – and so I was reading it and...one of the things I really like about *us*...is our passion. For answering important questions. Not just questions about ourselves but about the world and... I don't ever want to be the one who stands in the way of that, you know?

(She starts kissing his neck, unbuttoning his shirt...)

(As the Dark Figure slowly shrinks behind them.)

Everything alright?

SIMONA. Why wouldn't it be?

JAKE. You're just...um...

SIMONA. Remember what you said about how sometimes talking can spoil the moment?

JAKE. About that, I'm really sorry for –

SIMONA. How about we test that theory out?

(She kisses him. Aggressively. But this time, she seems content to let him take the lead when the moment is right.)

(And when he does, the Dark Figure doesn't loom large at all.)

(In fact, it's just the faintest flicker behind them.)

(So faint we hardly even notice it.)

(And finally, when he finishes...when he falls asleep in her arms...she's able to lie beneath his weight, feel him on top of her and not panic.)

(At least at first.)

(But after a moment, as he slumbers on top of her, as she caresses his hair, the Dark Figure starts to grow.)

(Slowly at first. And then more rapidly.)

(At which point, she pulls a pill bottle from the bedside table, pops the top, slips a pill in her mouth, swallows...)

(Banishing the Dark Figure from her mind for just a bit more.)

*(Then **JAKE** vanishes.)*

*(And her **ADVISER** appears.)*

ADVISER. Simona.

(She's not expecting him to be there, but realizes he must be there for a reason. So she approaches.)

SIMONA. You wanted to see me?

ADVISER. That last lab report you submitted was riddled with errors. Computational errors I'd maybe expect from an undergrad. But from you?

SIMONA. I...don't know what to say, Dr. Gardner.

ADVISER. What you ought to say is thank you. To Anthony. Who spotted the errors before they were put into the computer and compromised our results.

SIMONA. And he's sure I was the one who made the errors?

ADVISER. You were the only one working that day.

(Beat.)

SIMONA. *(Chastened.)* I'm sorry, Dr. Gardner. I promise you it won't happen again –

ADVISER. Are you alright, Simona?

SIMONA. I'm fine.

ADVISER. You're getting sleep?

SIMONA. Yes.

ADVISER. You're taking *care* of yourself?

SIMONA. I...am.

ADVISER. That's why you're struggling to stay awake in my class Thursday mornings?

> *(No answer.)*

Don't think that just because you show extraordinary promise the same rules don't apply to you.

SIMONA. I wouldn't think that, Dr. Gardner.

ADVISER. Then I expect you'll find it fair if I take you off my lab team. Pending your performance on your oral qual exams next month.

SIMONA. If that's what you think is best.

ADVISER. What would have been best is if you'd been focused enough to not record erroneous results. But clearly that's too much responsibility for you to handle right now. And clearly...you need to sort some things out.

> *(The **ADVISER** vanishes.)*

Ten

SIMONA. At least she's actually getting some sleep, right?

Maybe not much – definitely not enough – but still some. So...at least she's not lying when she tells him that much.

That small moral victory allows her to feel more than justified in continuing to burn the wick at both ends – cramming for her imminent quals and preemptively medicating for her intimate encounters with Jake.

I mean, because mistakes happen. Erroneous figures get recorded from time to time. And who can really say why? Who can really pin down the precise reason? The relationship between her new habit and her mistake in the lab? Purely correlational.

But the ability to not see the Dark Figure? Well, who can argue with that?

(**JAKE** *appears. The two of them dance.*)

(*At first it is tender, though intense.*)

(*But it quickly turns into something wilder. Far beyond* **SIMONA**'s *control.*)

(*So far beyond her control that she almost tumbles to the ground...*)

(*When* **JAKE** *catches her. At the last minute.*)

(*Covering with a smile.*) Whoops.

JAKE. Everything alright?

SIMONA. Guess I just got a little light-headed.

JAKE. Maybe I should get you some water –

SIMONA. No, no need, I can...

(She pulls herself to her feet, starts off.)

JAKE. If you're not feeling well you shouldn't be –

SIMONA. I said I'm feeling fine. And I'll be right back. So long as you promise you'll wait for me.

(She heads to the bathroom, turns on the faucet to mask the sound of opening drawers while she goes for her pills.)

(Only they're nowhere to be found.)

(So she starts rooting around feverishly.)

JAKE. You OK in there?

*(But **SIMONA** doesn't hear him. She's so fixated on finding what she lost.)*

Simona?

(Still no answer.)

If you need me to come in there –

SIMONA. *(On edge.)* I said I'm fine, didn't I?

JAKE. Well I apologize for being worried after you nearly passed out in my arms.

SIMONA. I'm sorry. I didn't mean to sound so defensive. It's sweet that you're worried.

(Giving up on her search in the bathroom.)

But you really don't need to be. Because...

(Swinging the bathroom door open.)

...I'm fine, see?

I just need to go ahead and grab something from the kitchen before we –

JAKE. Grab what?

SIMONA. Just...something I forgot.

JAKE. These?

(He holds up the bottle of her pills.)

I found them on the kitchen floor. And I wasn't sure if they were yours or your roommate's since they don't have anyone's name on them.

(She takes a quick step to grab them, but just as quickly stops herself.)

SIMONA. They're um...what are they?

JAKE. Psychotropics from what I can tell.

SIMONA. Oh then they're definitely hers. My roommate's. So if you just...I can take them and make sure she gets them –

(She goes for the bottle, but he doesn't hand it over.)

JAKE. Or maybe we should just flush them down the toilet and pretend like we never found them if she asks about it.

SIMONA. What?

JAKE. They're a highly-controlled substance that she shouldn't have without a prescription.

SIMONA. Or maybe we shouldn't be so fucking condescending by deciding why someone should or shouldn't need them.

(Silence.)

JAKE. So they're not your roommate's.

SIMONA. Of course they're...didn't I just say they were –

JAKE. Then why are you defending her?

SIMONA. I'm just saying you have no idea why someone would –

JAKE. Carry around prescription drugs in an unmarked bottle? It's not a long list of reasons. And I didn't know you were such a libertarian on that issue.

SIMONA. Well maybe that's because you just don't know me.

JAKE. That is...starting to become clear.

SIMONA. I told you: they're not mine.

JAKE. Then you shouldn't mind if I do this.

(He heads toward the toilet.)

(And, as much as she'd like to be able to let him flush them...that's just beyond her control right now.)

SIMONA. Don't.

(Pause.)

JAKE. I was hoping, praying that this sudden change in you was just because... I don't know, I had...or *we* had found...some...

But now that I say it out loud it sounds so ridiculous...

SIMONA. It's not.

JAKE. Really? When I caught my girlfriend sneaking off to the bathroom to take these every time we're about to be together?

SIMONA. There's an explanation.

JAKE. I'm waiting.

(Pause.)

SIMONA. It has nothing to do with you.

JAKE. Oh my God you have no idea how much I hope that's true.

SIMONA. You just...you have to trust me.

JAKE. No. You have to trust me enough to explain it.

SIMONA. *You're not the reason.*

JAKE. Then what is?

> *(She tries to speak. She really does.)*
>
> *(But then she sees the Dark Figure behind* **JAKE** *...and can't say anything...)*
>
> *(He leaves, takes the bottle with him.)*
>
> *(Leaving her nothing but her guilt, her sorrow...)*
>
> *(And the Dark Figure, which starts to grow again in Jake's absence.)*
>
> *(***SIMONA*** now has nothing to guard against him.)*
>
> *(All she can do is crouch to the floor and cradle herself...)*
>
> *(While the Dark Figure expands...overtakes the space...)*

Eleven

(When **SIMONA** *wakes up, she's in a hospital bed...)*

(And **PAPI** *is at her side, holding out a juice box.)*

PAPI. Fruit punch?

SIMONA. Where am I?

PAPI. Fruit punch first. Questions after. You're parched.

> *(She suddenly realizes the taste in her mouth is vile. That she is indeed parched.)*
>
> *(She takes the fruit punch, begins sucking it down.)*
>
> *(As soon as she does, he pulls out another juice box, spears it with a straw.)*

Tell me when you need another. I have a whole stash.

> *(He opens a small backpack at his side to reveal it filled to the brim with juice boxes.)*

I steal them from the nurse's station when she's not looking. She thinks I'm very charming, the nurse.

> *(Even in her current state – bedbound and straw between her lips –* **SIMONA** *can't help but smile at her father's antics.)*
>
> *(As soon as she finishes the juice box, as soon as we can hear her sucking on air,* **PAPI** *pries it from her hands and replaces it with another.)*

OK. Now questions.

SIMONA. Where am I?

PAPI. The hospital.

SIMONA. But...how?

PAPI. Your roommate found you. Passed out.

SIMONA. Oh shit...

PAPI. I guess you'd worked yourself to exhaustion studying for your –

SIMONA. Quals. My qual exams are –

PAPI. Were yesterday.

When I went to go get some of your things, there was a message from your adviser. Saying you'd missed them. That he wanted to talk about your future in the program.

Twelve

(The apartment.)

*(**PAPI** deftly dodges the ever-present stacks of science articles as he wheels Simona's suitcase into the space.)*

*(**SIMONA** follows him in, sinks into a chair, takes in the clutter.)*

*(**PAPI** is his usual self – buoyant, whistling, feet hovering three feet off the ground...)*

(All of which is a bit too much for her to take at the moment.)

SIMONA. You seem chipper.

(He stops, looks at her.)

PAPI. I know this is not how you wanted things to turn out, but we have to learn to look at it as a blessing.

SIMONA. I thought you didn't believe in blessings.

PAPI. I don't mean a religious blessing, *mi vida*, I just mean...we have to learn to look at the positive.

SIMONA. The positive of my mental breakdown.

PAPI. That's not –

SIMONA. Of my getting kicked out of my program.

PAPI. Being put on break.

SIMONA. He was being diplomatic. It looks bad if they kick people out. But I sincerely doubt he's hoping he'll see me again.

PAPI. Look, *mi vida*, my point is we can't know the reason why this had to happen, but if we learn to look at it the right way –

SIMONA. You mean your way.

PAPI. Not my way, *mi vida*. The right –

SIMONA. Because you're glad this happened, aren't you?

PAPI. That's...how could you think I'd be glad –

SIMONA. You never wanted me to go there in the first place. You never wanted me to take a single step down this path. So this – my being here – it vindicates you.

PAPI. *Mi vida* –

SIMONA. And that's what you mean when you say we should learn to look at the positive. You mean we should both be happy because you were right.

PAPI. I don't know what you're talking about, *mi vida*.

SIMONA. You think I did this to myself.

PAPI. What?

SIMONA. That's what you're thinking.

PAPI. When did I ever say that?

SIMONA. You didn't have to.

PAPI. All I've done is come to be by your side, try my best to take care of you –

SIMONA. But you're still convinced I brought it on myself.

PAPI. I'm not sure what you want from me, Simona.

SIMONA. To tell me the truth.

PAPI. The truth is that you're my daughter and I love you very much and it hurts me very much to see you like this.

SIMONA. But it's still my fault that I'm here.

(*Beat.*)

PAPI. If that's how you feel then there's not much I can do about it, is there? We both know how stubborn you are when you've set your mind on something.

SIMONA. But you're not arguing with me because you agree.

PAPI. Because I'm not sure what good it will do.

SIMONA. Then at least say it.

PAPI. But I never said –

(She grabs him forcefully.)

SIMONA. At least have the decency to say the words out loud! –

PAPI. *Mi vida* –

SIMONA. That I brought all this on myself –

PAPI. But –

SIMONA. That it's all my fault. That if I'd just had the good sense to listen to you and do something sensible with my life – that if I weren't so fucking fragile that I can't even seem to survive the simple, privileged life you've handed me when so many people who've been through so much worse don't crumble like stale fucking toast at the barest hint of adversity or...or...or...

(Her anger soon gives way to tears as she collapses onto him.)

(But he doesn't grab her. Or hold her up.)

(Instead he just stands there, overwhelmed, as she slowly crumples to the floor.)

(He just stands over her, not sure what to do.)

(The most he can muster is a tentative pat on the head.)

Thirteen

(The piles of papers appear all around her.)

SIMONA. Sitting on her bed

surrounded by old science articles her father still hasn't picked up

too terrified of her dreams to even think about sleeping

the little girl does the only thing she can.

> *(She plucks articles from the piles of paper around her...and reads.)*

> *(We hear a beep.)*

> *(And **JAKE** appears in another part of the space.)*

JAKE. Hey. It's me. I um...I got your home number from your roommate. In case you're wondering how I...

I came by your place to check on you the day after our... disagreement. And she told me you weren't around. That you weren't going to be around any time soon. And I guess you'd never told her we were dating? Because it took a while to convince her I wasn't just some creep who was stalking you so...by the time I finally found out you were in the hospital...you were gone.

Anyway, I'm just calling to check on you. And to see if maybe you'd want me to come visit? Or –

> *(Another beep.)*

> *(She continues reading.)*

SIMONA. She shuts out the world

and tries to drown out the Dark Figure

with the beauty

and abstraction

of quarks and quasars...

JAKE. Hey Simona, it's Jake again. I'm not sure if you got my message the first time, so I figured I'd try again.

SIMONA. ...of distant galaxies collapsing in on themselves and unfolding again...

> *(We see the silhouettes of distant galaxies and solar systems intermingling on the scrim...)*
>
> *(They somewhat obscure our view of the Dark Figure...)*

JAKE. But if you did get it and just didn't have time to answer it... Or if my calling you like this is annoying or... I'm intruding on your personal space or whatever, please feel free to call me and tell me off.

SIMONA. On the most colossal things the human mind has been able to fathom...

JAKE. I totally won't be offended. I just want to make sure you're –

> *(Beep.)*

SIMONA. And on the most minuscule...

JAKE. Just a word. Or a message with the sound of you breathing on the other end of the line if a word's too much. Or the sound of your scribbling pen. Or... anything. I'd be so grateful for anything. Even if it's the last I hear from you. Because I'm human. And I care. And –

> *(Beep.)*
>
> *(**JAKE** vanishes.)*

SIMONA. And in the midst of this binge

the little girl suddenly finds her salvation

in the most unexpected place.

(A giant rat appears in the center of the space.)

Not an actual, literal rat...

(Or rather, a man in a giant rat suit.)

...but a lab rat.

*(And by a man in a giant rat suit I mean **JAKE** wearing rat ears and a tail.)*

Technically, a legion of lab rats. Who had been exposed to the sweet, aromatic smell of cherry blossoms...

*(The **RAT/JAKE** indulges in the smell...)*

Ah, cherry blossoms...

(He practically bathes in the aroma as it wafts through the space in a cloud of pink mist...)

Only to receive an electric shock...

*(The **RAT/JAKE**'s hair suddenly stands on end as an electric shock courses through his body.)*

...accompanying the smell each and every time.

The experimenters repeated this pattern

Cherry blossom

Shock

Cherry blossom

Shock

Cherry blossom

Shock...

> *(We watch the* **RAT/JAKE** *delight in the aromatic smell anew...)*

> *(And be surprised each time that the electric shock immediately bites him in the ass...)*

...until the poor little rats became terrified

their tiny hearts throbbing at the mere trace of cherry blossom...

> *(...Until the repeated pattern takes its toll on the poor* **RAT/JAKE.***)*

> *(And he's nothing more than a twitching puddle of fur and fear.)*

And then the experimenters let the poor, traumatized rats procreate!

> *(Party time! Suddenly the* **RAT/JAKE** *is shaking that tail with reckless abandon...)*

And raise their offspring into adulthood...

Then, and only then, did the experimenters expose this new generation of rats to the smell of cherry blossoms. To see what would happen.

And, well, as soon as the second generation rats experienced that most magical smell...

> *(The* **RAT/JAKE** *is instantly reduced to the twitching puddle once again.)*

"But how could that be?" The experimenters wondered

since these new rats had never encountered the smell of cherry blossoms?

How could these rats be so afraid of something they'd never experienced?

Something rats as a species had not evolved to be afraid of?

The natural explanation would be that their traumatized parents had taught them to fear the loathsome smell.

And yet their parents never had an occasion to teach them.

So the only answer that remained

was that their traumatic response had somehow been passed down through their blood.

Encoded in their DNA.

> *(Tinny tango music filters in the background as* **SIMONA** *approaches the* **RAT/JAKE**...**)*
>
> *(Offers him a hand... Helps him off the floor...)*
>
> *(As she starts to dance with him...)*
>
> *(The* **RAT/JAKE** *speaks. With a French accent.)*

RAT. I must admit. I never could've imagined a woman as radiant and potent as you having any attraction to a rodent as vile and filthy as me.

SIMONA. Never underestimate the power of being the one man in a woman's life who makes her feel less crazy.

RAT. You're sure you're not just leading me on? Like all the others?

SIMONA. Others?

---

* A license to produce *Simona's Search* does not include a performance license for any third-party or copyrighted recordings. Licensees should create their own.

RAT. You think you're the first gloved hand who's reached in my cage?

> *(Beat.)*

You can't imagine how many times I stared across the wire-mesh divide, just hoping, praying that the white-coated object of my affection might notice me. Of course all the other rats tell me I'm a fool. That she's a renowned scientist and you're just a filthy rodent. That there's *no way*. How could a rat and a human *ever...*? How could we poor rodents ever overcome the stigma of the bubonic plague? But I ignore them. Keep blinking at her with pink, expectant eyes. 'Til one day it seems as if my dreams might come true. She picks me up – *me*, of *all* the rats – plucks me from my cage oh-so-tenderly...caresses me...steadies my little, throbbing heart...

But inevitably my dreams are dashed with a cold pin-prick, some crippling side effects, and eventually...*la chambre à gaz.*

SIMONA. I'm different. You mean something to me.

RAT. I always mean something, chérie. Numbers. Data.

SIMONA. To me you mean more. You mean...knowing I'm not alone. That there are others out there like me. People haunted by a past they've never lived. And if we know why they are the way they are, why I am the way I am – if we know these people aren't just crazy...then there's hope.

> *(He's trying his best to understand what she's saying, but it's just beyond the poor guy.)*

> *(He is a **RAT**, after all.)*

They say our anatomies are more similar than you might think.

> Similar organs
>
> nervous systems
>
> reactions to injury and infections
>
> similar hormones...

RAT. *(Intrigued.)* Now we're talking...

SIMONA. And here I am, hoping your body maps perfectly onto mine...

RAT. Tell me more.

SIMONA. You see if your body's a perfect mirror of mine... then what happened to you when you smelled the cherry blossom –

RAT. Unless you're deliberately trying to kill the mood I'll kindly ask you to refrain from mentioning that dreaded flower ever again.

> *(Suddenly, he notices her mind is elsewhere.)*

Something on your mind?

SIMONA. You see? We *are* in sync!

RAT. *(Trying to nudge her back in the right direction.)* Tell me how.

SIMONA. I was just wondering how the article – your article – wound up in the pile in my bedroom. When everything else is about physics and theoretical math, why would he include an article about biology? Genetics?

RAT. Maybe it was on the back of another article? Something about string theory or the like?

SIMONA. No, it was definitely the main article. He clipped it out very carefully.

RAT. Maybe he clipped it by mistake? Thought he was cutting out something else and –

SIMONA. Unless he slipped it in the pile on purpose. As his way of telling me what I'm studying really matters.

RAT. Why wouldn't he just come right out and say it?

SIMONA. Um...you clearly don't know my father.

RAT. Human psychology is so exhausting.

SIMONA. Do you think it's possible, though? That he put it in there as a way of telling me something he wasn't ready to openly admit?

RAT. How the hell am I supposed to know? I'm just a rat.

SIMONA. But I thought you were... I thought we were in sync!

RAT. Not until you can prove we are.

SIMONA. But...but –

(A knock on the door.)

*(**PAPI** appears. The **RAT/JAKE** vanishes.)*

PAPI. You need something, *mi vida?*

(No answer.)

I heard you talking. I thought you might have been asking for me.

SIMONA. I was talking.

PAPI. To me?

SIMONA. ...

PAPI. Is there something you wanted to ask me, Simona?

(The slightest hesitation...)

SIMONA. No. I was just...thinking aloud.

Fourteen

SIMONA. She writes the study's lead author

explains her situation

her credentials

her personal connection to the study's line of inquiry

and asks for a job

any job

even if it means sweeping floors

gassing rats and disposing of their little corpses in a
furnace

any job that might contribute in some small way

to the creation of knowledge so powerful.

She writes this email on a lark

sure it's headed straight for Dr. Nusbaum's spam folder.

So naturally she's shocked to receive a reply within
forty-eight hours

inviting her to interview

not as a janitor

but as a bona fide research assistant.

She tells her father she's going to visit a friend from
college

blow off some steam she says

before packing her bags for the interview

where she's offered a job

a generous stipend

and a position in the lab's new PhD program.

As soon as she starts working in the lab –

> *(Suddenly she sees **PAPI**. Standing there. Reading the article.)*

> *(She looks at him like maybe he shouldn't be there. Before repeating...)*

As soon as she starts *working in the lab...*

> *(But **PAPI** just stands there. Oblivious. Studying the article.)*

> *(She clears her throat, which doesn't seem to register with him...)*

PAPI. I don't understand.

> *(She looks at us, not quite sure what to do.)*

I do not understand...

> *(She looks at us one more time, makes a decision to engage with **PAPI**.)*

SIMONA. *(To **PAPI**.)* If you want I can explain it again –

PAPI. I understand the experiment, *mi vida* – the sniffing, and the cherry blossoms, and their throbbing little hearts... I just don't understand why you're telling me.

SIMONA. This is what I'm going to be studying.

PAPI. What happens to rats when they sniff cherry blossoms. A frivolous thing to be studying when you've barely had any time to rest –

SIMONA. I'm studying what that might mean for humans.

> *(Back to us.)*

So. As soon as she starts working in the lab –

PAPI. Nothing.

(She looks at him.)

PAPI. It means nothing. A rat is a rat and a person is a person and aside from bubonic plague, a rat has nothing to offer –

SIMONA. Even if I'm sure I've experienced what that article describes?

(He looks at her, needing an explanation.)

(She knows the only way is through.)

My...breakdown. I told you it was because I was tired. Overworked.

PAPI. That's what the doctor said.

SIMONA. I was too afraid to tell him the real reason.

What I see every time I shut my eyes.

(The Dark Figure appears.)

*(**PAPI** sees it, recognizes it right away, tries hard to hide his anxiety.)*

PAPI. Since when?

*(In the background, we hear a distorted version of the folk song – the haunting melody – **SIMONA** listened to all those years ago.*)*

SIMONA. Since I was fourteen.

For the longest time I thought I'd done it to myself. That my own curiosity, my own desire to understand you, had made me...

---

*A license to produce *Simona's Search* does not include a performance license for any third-party or copyrighted recordings. Licensees should create their own.

PAPI. But now you feel better because you can blame it on me.

SIMONA. Who said anything about blame?

PAPI. Isn't that what you're saying? That it's all my fault?

SIMONA. No more than it's your fault that we both have brown eyes. Or…if we both had the gene for Alzheimer's or glaucoma…

And if you knew you had those genes…if you knew I might have them, too…wouldn't you want me to know?

(He says nothing.)

What this study means…is your business is my business. Your business has worked its way into me and made itself my business.

PAPI. So I'm supposed to tell you what that business is?

SIMONA. You can't cure an illness if you don't know the cause.

(He looks at her…)

(At the Dark Figure…)

(Which looms larger than ever.)

You know it's true, Papi, or you'd have never left me that article.

PAPI. I didn't leave it.

SIMONA. There's no other way it would've gotten in that pile so neatly cut out –

PAPI. I don't know how it got there, *mi vida*, but I know it didn't come from me. And neither did what you're seeing.

(She looks at him.)

SIMONA. Think about what you're saying, Papi...

PAPI. I have thought about it.

SIMONA. If you're really saying it doesn't come from you, then you're saying that I...invented it or I'm crazy –

PAPI. If the only other option is it came from me, that's exactly what I'm saying.

  (Beat.)

SIMONA. I don't believe you really think that –

  (He explodes –)

PAPI. I do think it!

  (Silence.)

You did this, Simona.

I'm not touching a hot stove and complaining it hurts.

  (PAPI *vanishes.)*

  (So does the Dark Figure.)

  (SIMONA *is left alone. In shock.)*

Fifteen

(**SIMONA** *stands there in silence for the longest moment...*)

(*Trying to summon the strength to speak...*)

(*For the first time, we wonder whether she'll actually be able to. Or whether she'll just give up and walk off. Leave us alone. The story incomplete.*)

(*But eventually she manages to tell us...*)

SIMONA. That's the last substantive conversation I have with my father for almost two years.

We spend the rest of my time at home barely acknowledging the other exists

until it's time for me to start the next chapter of my life.

The research

my colleagues

the support of my new mentor

is exactly what I dreamed it'd be.

And while definitive proof that humans pass down genetic markers of their trauma remains elusive...

We uncover compelling evidence that points us in that direction.

Cross-sectional studies of different refugee communities reveal American-born children who suffer from the same trauma-related afflictions as their parents and grandparents – even though these children have no specific knowledge of what happened to their parents and grandparents.

I interview these children. From their own life circumstances, they have every reason to be happy. Healthy. Well-adjusted.

But they still have a whole host of anxiety and depression disorders lurking silently beneath the surface.

And while it breaks my heart to listen to all these young people carrying secret burdens they have no way to comprehend...

...it also comforts me.

Knowing I'm not alone.

And I'm not the only one who feels this way.

One day in the lab

one of the subjects I'm interviewing

is so relieved to hear others experience her same symptoms

that she grabs me

hugs me...

It's the first time someone's held me like this since...

and the dark figure

he's still right there

but for the first time

I start to see the faintest hint of his features inside that silhouette

the contour of his nose

the arch of his eyebrows

maybe even the whites of his eyes...
That night I sleep better than I have in years. The next night, too.

So I decide to do something I'm sure will shed light on the Dark Figure once and for all.

I book a flight to my father's homeland for the first time in my life.

I go find the old songs I listened to on those cassettes from the library...

> *(We hear the folk song echo through the space...[*])*

And soon after I send my father my flight info

ask if there's anything I should see.

No answer.

But as I count down the days to my trip

I'm more and more certain with each day

that before I step on that plane

he'll call and say...what, exactly? I'm not sure

something to break the wall of silence between us.

The calendar by my bed

becomes a countdown to that call as much as anything

and the more he makes me wait for it

the more certain I am the call is coming

until my flight is just forty hours away –

> *(Rrrrrrriiiiiing!)*

> **(SIMONA** *races to the phone.)*

> *(But the number is not what she expected.)*

(*She hesitates a moment, decides to pick up anyway.*)

(*A* **DOCTOR** *appears.*)

DOCTOR. Hi. Is this Ms. Cruz?

SIMONA. This is she. May I ask who's –

DOCTOR. Dr. Frazier from Covenant Hospital. We have your father here.

(*Lights flash.*)

(**SIMONA** *is flanked on either side by the* **DOCTOR**...)

(*...And* **PAPI** *in his hospital bed...*)

(*...Each in his own pool of light.*)

To call your father's case complex would be an understatement.

PAPI. Can someone tell me what I'm doing here!?

DOCTOR. His blood pressure's sky-high, kidney function's compromised –

PAPI. They've had me in this ridiculous place for *fifteen hours* –

DOCTOR. He doubles over in severe pain every time he tries to walk –

PAPI. – when the doctor himself said it:

DOCTOR. But we keep running tests and we can't seem to find –

PAPI.	**DOCTOR.**
There's nothing wrong with me!	– anything wrong with him.

DOCTOR. Until we do find something, I'm not comfortable releasing him. But...if we can't find something definitive, I'm not sure what else we can do.

(The **DOCTOR** *vanishes, leaving* **SIMONA** *alone with* **PAPI**.*)*

PAPI. *Mi vida.* Quick. Go find the doctor and explain to him how he has to let me go because there's nothing wrong with me. He'll listen to you as a medical professional –

SIMONA. I'm a neuroscience researcher. I doubt he'll consider them the same.

PAPI. You never know until you try. So go and tell him. Remind him that he said it himself. There's nothing wrong with me –

SIMONA. And I already talked to him.

Just because they can't find anything wrong doesn't mean it's not there.

It just means they have to keep looking.

PAPI. Fine. If you're not going to help...

(He starts to get out of his bed.)

SIMONA. *(Trying to stop him.)* Papi, please –

(But before he can get very far, he doubles over in pain.)

Papi, what's wrong?

PAPI. Nothing. Nothing. I told you there's nothing...

(She helps him back to his hospital bed, where he catches his breath.)

SIMONA. *(As she turns to us.)* Needless to say, I don't get on the plane.

SIMONA. I don't go to the airport

or even leave the hospital.

I sit by my father's bed

trying to keep his spirits up

while he rants and raves…

       (**PAPI** *rants and raves from his hospital bed.*)

While the doctors run their tests

and any definitive answer about what's wrong with my father

continues to elude them.

Until one day my father's symptoms miraculously subside…

       (**PAPI** *throws the covers off himself and leaps out of bed in a single, swift, acrobatic motion. Ta-dah!*)

…so the doctors send him home

scratching their heads

I return to my research

and we forget all about his mysterious hospital stay…

Until I reschedule my trip.

And, sure enough, within forty-eight hours of my departure…

       (*Brrrrrrriiiiiing!*)

DOCTOR. Ms. Cruz, your father's back in.

       (**PAPI***'s back in his hospital bed.*)

SIMONA. And once again I miss my flight

to sit by my father's side

while he rants and raves

while the doctors run their tests

more mystified than before

until my father makes an equally miraculous recovery...

> (**PAPI** *once again makes his acrobatic leap out of bed...*)

Except this time it's not a complete recovery.

> (*But this time* **PAPI** *is visibly more stooped than he was before.*)

This time my father seems to lose a step.

It's the same with his next hospital stay.

> (*We watch as* **PAPI** *becomes more stooped...*)

And the one after that.

> (*... And more stooped.*)

Each coming within hours of my scheduled departure.

I'm sure by now you're thinking the same thing I did.

That his illness is just an act.

> (*She looks at her stooped* **PAPI**.)

So you should probably know that the last two times I reschedule my trip

I don't tell him

or anyone but my boss

make sure there's no way my father will know

and still

forty hours before lift off...

(Brrrrrriiiiing...)

So I give up on my trip

immerse myself in my research.

But my father doesn't get better

The hospital visits just become an accumulation of doctor's appointments.

> *(The **DOCTOR** appears in silhouette behind the stooped **PAPI**...who still wears his hospital gown.)*

> *(As the **DOCTOR** "examines" **PAPI** by poking and prodding him in increasingly invasive ways...)*

> *(The **DOCTOR** starts to resemble the Dark Figure...)*

> *(So much so that we think he may actually be the Dark Figure...)*

For two years I watch the life leak out of my father...

> *(The **DOCTOR** vanishes...)*

> *(Leaving behind a shell of the man that once was.)*

Until it becomes clear that time is running out

and all the specialists in the world won't solve the puzzle.

Sixteen

*(**SIMONA** quickly brings **PAPI** a chair, which he's all too happy to fall into.)*

(Then she brings him a bowl and spoon…)

(And watches him eat. With great effort.)

SIMONA. I know what's wrong.

(He looks up from his soup.)

(Even something as simple as lifting his head seems to require extra effort.)

With you. I know what's wrong with you.

PAPI. There's a lot wrong with me, *mi vida.* So much it takes a whole team of men to start to tell you.

SIMONA. But none of them can tell you why.

PAPI. And you can?

(She nods. He considers this a moment. Then…)

I thought you weren't a medical professional. So what is it you could know that they don't?

(Beat.)

(She considers a moment whether to say it…)

SIMONA. *Tu pasado.* (Your past.)

*(We're sure a younger, more energetic version of **PAPI** would find some way to weasel out of the topic at hand. Or avoid the subject altogether.)*

(But he no longer has the energy for that. Nor does he have the time.)

PAPI. And you think that has something to do with –

SIMONA. I know it does.

(More silence. An invitation to continue.)

We get people like you in the lab all the time. People who've suffered. So much that they can't even begin to say. But all those years holding it in…and the suffering starts to express itself in other ways. In sickness that eats away at the body for no apparent reason –

PAPI. I –

SIMONA. Before you say anything…this is not my way of getting you to talk.

I've given up on that. And not because I don't want to know. I do. But… I've also seen enough people who… talking only makes it worse.

And I strongly suspect you are one of them.

PAPI. Then why are you…?

SIMONA. Because there's something I think can help.

A drug some of my colleagues are working on that can…take a traumatic memory and rob it of its pain.

(He can't help but laugh.)

I know it sounds like magic – it almost is magic – but I promise you it's real.

They are making a drug that can work its way into the brain so that when you bring a traumatic memory back to life…we can starve it of its fear. Slowly starve it to death.

All that's left is to test it.

PAPI. And you want me.

SIMONA. I couldn't be a part of the study if you volunteered.

But I'd be willing to do that for you.

Because I think this could give us some more time.

(Long silence.)

PAPI. *¿Nunca te ha ocurrido, mi vida…que es posible que yo quiera mi dolor?* (Has it ever occurred to you, *mi vida*…that I might want my pain?)

SIMONA. *Pero está matándote, Papi –* (But it's killing you, Papi –)

PAPI. *Eso no quiere decir que me equivoco.* (That doesn't mean I'm not right.)

(Beat.)

My pain is how I know we were wronged. The only way anyone will know.

SIMONA. It doesn't have to be the only way –

PAPI. I could do nothing but tell them for the next thousand years. They still wouldn't know.

(Beat.)

So no. I will not take your drug.

(Another beat. He rests a hand on hers.)

Besides… I wouldn't dream of taking your spot in that experiment away from you.

(He turns back to his soup…)

SIMONA. *(As she turns to us.)* From that day forward, my father stopped going to the doctor.

Which I think was his way of admitting he'd known all along what was killing him.

His way of admitting I was right before he died...

Which he did within the year.

But not before...

>(**PAPI** *lies there in his bed. By now he wears an oxygen mask and can no longer summon enough breath to speak.*)

>(**SIMONA** *sits by his side, not saying anything either. They just silently enjoy each other's company.*)

>(*Until she says...*)

Thank you.

>(*He looks at her. His expression hovers between confused and incredulous.*)

I mean it. Thank you.

>(*As best he can, he shrugs his shoulders, as if to say: "What for?"*)

You did a good job.

>(*He keeps looking at her, not quite sure he believes her.*)

You did.

>(*Another moment's silence.*)

>(*Then suddenly he extends his hand.*)

>(*She looks at it for a second, not quite sure why it's hanging there like that. But she goes out on a limb and takes his hand in hers. As soon as she does, she realizes this is exactly what he wanted.*)

(They go right back to silently enjoying each other's company.)

(Until she turns to us...)

The day after he passes...

*(**PAPI** suddenly gets up, as if he remembered something he'd forgotten. As he shuffles offstage to get it, oxygen tank in tow, he accidentally knocks over his soup...)*

(And we listen to both bowl and spoon clang noisily on the floor...)

(...before they finally come to a rest.)

...I open his will to find out he's donated his body to science.

The instant I sign it over to the hospital

I begin a frantic search through his papers

for something he may have left behind

something he wanted me to know but was too afraid to say while he was alive...

Only to stop. After a few minutes. Wonder if that's really what I want.

Or if after so many years of searching it's just a stubborn habit...

So I call my boss

ask for time off

and I book that trip

the one I'd been meaning to take

to...fill in the contours of the Dark Figure once and for all?

Maybe.

But not by looking straight at him this time.

By learning to glance away every once in a while

by sitting in a café

talking to a random stranger on the street

breathing the same air my father used to breathe

listening to the same songs he heard

when he was a young man who didn't know what worries were...

> *(We hear the folk song once again. It's clearer this time. More vibrant.*)*

> **(SIMONA** *sways to the music, unashamed. Perhaps even proud.)*

And if, after all that, the little girl looks back at the Dark Figure

and he's just as hazy as before?

Maybe that's because he's not meant to be filled in all the way.

And maybe she'll have to learn to live with that.

> *(The Dark Figure appears behind her. Or at least what's left of it.)*

> *(We almost think we can make out its features, but this seems to rob it of its clear contours...)*

---

* A license to produce *Simona's Search* does not include a performance license for any third-party or copyrighted recordings. Licensees should create their own.

(Makes its edges blurry to the point that we wonder if it even exists.)

End of Play